P9-CJD-339

P9-CJD-339

FOR MY DAUGHTER, SASHA, AND MY SON, KOSTYA.

Patricia Lee Gauch, Editor

PHILOMEL BOOKS
A division of Penguin Young Readers Group.
Published by The Penguin Group.
Penguin Group (USA) Inc., 375 Hudson Street, New York, NY 10014, U.S.A.
Penguin Group (Canada), 90 Eglinton Avenue East, Suite 700, Toronto, Ontario, Canada M4P 2Y3
    (a division of Pearson Penguin Canada Inc.).
Penguin Books Ltd, 80 Strand, London WC2R 0RL, England.
Penguin Ireland, 25 St. Stephen's Green, Dublin 2, Ireland (a division of Penguin Books Ltd.).
Penguin Group (Australia), 250 Camberwell Road, Camberwell, Victoria 3124, Australia (a division of
    Pearson Australia Group Pty Ltd).
Penguin Books India Pvt Ltd, 11 Community Centre, Panchsheel Park, New Delhi - 110 017, India.
Penguin Group (NZ), Cnr Airborne and Rosedale Roads, Albany, Auckland 1310, New Zealand
    (a division of Pearson New Zealand Ltd).
Penguin Books (South Africa) (Pty) Ltd, 24 Sturdee Avenue, Rosebank, Johannesburg 2196,
    South Africa.
Penguin Books Ltd, Registered Offices: 80 Strand, London WC2R 0RL, England.

Text set in 17-point Worcester Round Med.
Design by Semadar Megged.
The illustrations are rendered in pen-and-ink and watercolors.

Library of Congress Cataloging-in-Publication Data
Gorbachev, Valeri.
Heron and Turtle / Valeri Gorbachev.
p. cm.   Summary: Despite their differences, Heron and
Turtle are very good neighbors and friends.
[1. Best friends—Fiction. 2. Friendship—Fiction.
3. Neighbors—Fiction. 4. Turtles—Fiction.
5. Herons—Fiction.] I. Title.   PZ7.G6475Her 2006
[E]—dc22   2005019712

ISBN 0-399-24321-6
10 9 8 7 6 5 4 3 2 1
First Impression

HERON & TURTLE

Valeri Gorbachev

PHILOMEL BOOKS

TWO NEIGHBORS LIVED next to each other on the shore of Forest Lake.

One neighbor was Heron, the other neighbor was Turtle.

"Hello, Heron," neighbor Turtle would say, floating by in his boat. "How are you?"

"I'm fine, thank you," replied Heron. "And you?"

"I am fine, too," said Turtle.

They were good, good neighbors.

HOW HERON AND TURTLE WENT FOR A WALK TOGETHER

One lovely summer morning, neighbor Turtle stopped by his friend Heron's house.

"Good morning, Heron," said Turtle. "It is a beautiful day today. Would you like to go for a walk with me?"

"Yes," said Heron. "I love to walk in the morning."

"We can walk to the meadow," said Turtle, "then to the lake."

"Sounds good," said Heron.

"But, friend Heron," cried Turtle, "you go too fast.
Wait for me!"

"Where are you, Turtle?" Heron called.

"I am here," said Turtle. "But, friend Heron, you are still walking too fast."

"I am sorry, Turtle," said
Heron. "It is because I have very
long legs, and you have very short
legs. I will try to walk slower."

But in a moment, Turtle shouted, "Hey, Heron!
Wait up. You are going too fast again."

Heron sat down. "Turtle, I am so sorry. You are walking too slow, and I am walking too fast. How can we go for a walk together?"

"It isn't easy, but I have an idea,"
said Turtle.

"Come ride with me in my boat. You will have no trouble keeping up."

"What a good idea," said Heron. "I love floating in your boat with you on this beautiful summer morning."

HOW HERON VISITED TURTLE
ONE DAY

"Hello, Turtle," said Heron one afternoon. "I was just walking by your house and thought how nice it would be to stop by and see you."

"Come on in," said Turtle to his friend. "I am glad to see you, Heron!"

"Sorry for the unexpected visit," said Heron.

"That's okay," Turtle said. "I will fix a delicious
lunch for us."

"Just wait a second and everything will
be ready," Turtle said.

"Don't go to any trouble, dear Turtle," said Heron.

"I am sorry to keep you waiting," said Turtle.
"I hope you aren't bored."

"Not at all," said Heron.

"I am almost finished," said Turtle. "Just one last footstool . . ."

"Now everything is ready, Heron."
And the two friends sat down to lunch.
"Perfect," said Heron.
"I am so glad you visited me, Heron," said Turtle.

"I am glad that I visited you, too, Turtle," said Heron. "You are a very good friend."

"Thank you," said Turtle, "I try."

HOW TURTLE AND HERON WERE ENJOYING A SUMMER EVENING ON THE LAKE

One summer evening, Heron and Turtle were sitting on a log by the lake.

"I love sunset on the lake," said Heron.

"Me, too," said Turtle.

"I love listening to the choir of frogs
on our lake," said Heron.
"Me, too," said Turtle.

"I love the music of the pond," said Heron.
"Me, too," said Turtle.

"I love the moon in the sky and the stars mirrored in the water on the lake. And I love Beaver's boat floating between the stars and moon mirrored in the water on the lake," said Heron.

"Me, too," said Turtle.

"Would you like to know what else I love about this beautiful summer evening?" asked Turtle.

"Sure," said Heron, "I would love to know."

"I love enjoying this beautiful summer evening with you, Heron, my best friend," said Turtle.

"You are my best friend, too, Turtle," said Heron.

And they both watched the moon and the stars reflecting in the lake together, and smiled happily.